MW01143378

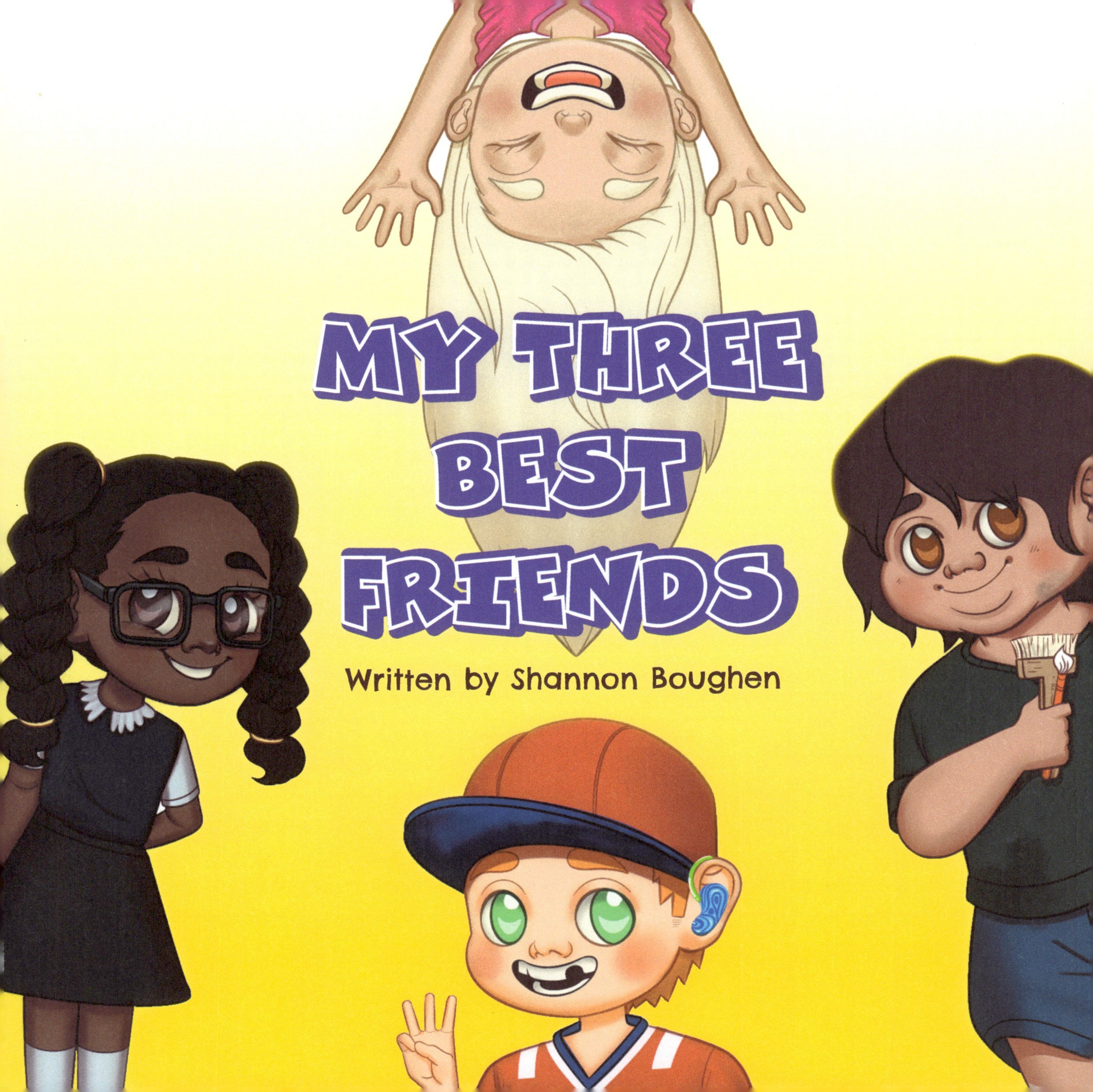
MY THREE BEST FRIENDS
Written by Shannon Boughen

Dedicated to my biggest supporters
Jared & Sadie

I want to introduce you to my three best friends...

Joey never ties his shoes.
Sadie never wears matching colours.
Amelia matches all the time.
I like to have my own style.

Sometimes when we get together, we're very loud!
Other times, we would rather have quiet time.
CHIPS
CHIPS
We share stories, crafts,
and tell funny jokes,
and there are always
lots of snacks!
We try to match our games
to our moods that day.

Joey draws on everything.
Sadie gets all the math questions right.
Amelia likes to read.
I only love sports.
SADIE
SOCCER
BASKET BALL
SPORTS IS LIFE
AMELIA

Joey sometimes needs help with reading, and Sadie always likes to try new things. So, Amelia helps Joey with his reading while I show Sadie my sports skills.
Sometimes she can play the game better than me.

Joey thinks talking is overrated.
Sadie doesn't stop talking.
Amelia giggles at everything.
I like to talk about sports.
SKETCHBOOK

I don't like it when Joey gets distracted easily,
or when Sadie never stops talking.
And when Amelia is feeling shy,
she doesn't want to go on adventures.
But on those days, I can play on my own,
or meet new friends at the playground.

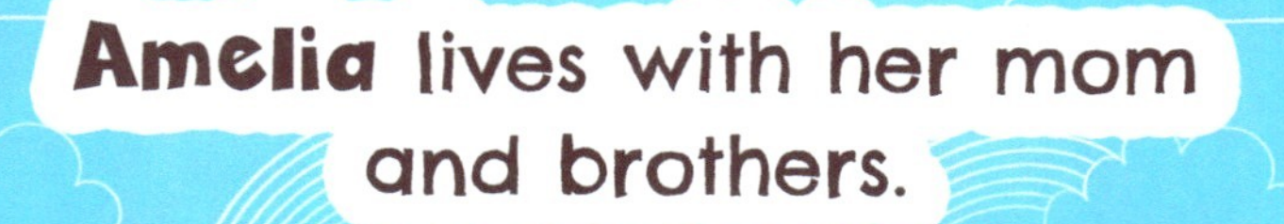

Amelia lives with her mom and brothers.

Joey lives with his grandma.

Sadie lives with her mom and dad; her siblings have moved out on their own.

I live with my dad.

When **Joey** misses his parents
or I miss my mom,
we visit **Sadie**'s brother
and sister on our bicycles.
Or we go to **Amelia**'s house–
MEOW
Amelia's house has so
many people
there is never a
dull moment!

Joey is bigger than me.
Sadie has long hair.
Amelia wears glasses.
I have hearing aids.

One time, when kids were making fun of how I looked,
Joey stood up for me and told them to stop.
Sadie gave me a hug
to make me feel better.
Amelia made me laugh again.
My best friends are amazing.

SKETCHBOOK
Joey only eats peanut butter sandwiches!
Sadie likes fruit best of all.
Amelia has soup every day,
and is allergic to a whole list of foods.
I eat whatever is in my lunch box.

One day, **Amelia** was sad because her lunch box didn't have a character on it, but **Sadie**'s lunch box had a pretty unicorn.
(My lunch box is plain blue, but I like it that way.)
Joey drew **Amelia** a princess and glued it onto her lunch box.
Amelia's smile at lunch was as big as the sun!

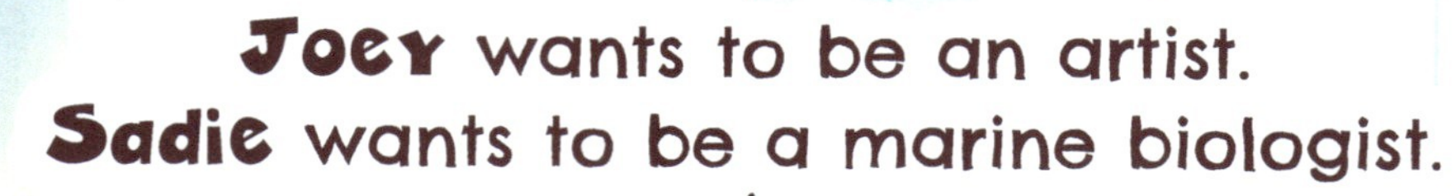

Joey wants to be an artist.
Sadie wants to be a marine biologist.

HORSE TRAINER
TEACHER
RACE CAR DRIVER
DOCTOR
SCIENTIST
FIGURE SKATER
Amelia wants to be a scientist, a race car driver, a horse trainer, a teacher, a doctor, a figure skater... it depends on the day!
I want to climb to the top of a mountain and travel the world.

I asked my friends, "If you had a superpower, what would your magic skill be?"

I want to be able to fly! It would make travelling to far off destinations easier and faster.

Joey wants to be able to paint a masterpiece and have everyone remember his name!

Amelia wants to eat whatever she wants without feeling sick.
Sadie wants to save every animal from harm...except snakes. She doesn't like snakes.

I have the best friends.
We have so many things that are the same—and
some that are different, too!
We have some disabilities,
and lots of abilities.
We laugh, we play, we dream...
and we know how to have fun!

I can't wait to see what tomorrow brings for me and **my three best friends.**

ABOUT THE AUTHOR

Shannon Boughen had a dream to write a children's book. Growing up in a small town, Goderich, Ontario allowed her to create many strong friendships. Shannon believes friendship means accepting people's differences, and supporting one another to help strengthen our weak spots. She feels life is about having fun, enjoying friends and family, and dreaming big!

One Printers Way
Altona, MB R0G 0B0
Canada

www.friesenpress.com

First Edition — 2024

ISBN
978-1-03-919452-6 (Hardcover)
978-1-03-919451-9 (Paperback)
978-1-03-919453-3 (eBook)

1. JUVENILE FICTION, SOCIAL ISSUES, VALUES & VIRTUES

Distributed to the trade by The Ingram Book Company

Printed in the USA
CPSIA information can be obtained
at www.ICGtesting.com
LVHW061832030424
776136LV00018B/39

* 9 7 8 1 0 3 9 1 9 4 5 2 6 *